MW00878382

The Promise

Dawn Comer Jefferson
Rosanne Welch

The Promise

Dawn Comer Jefferson
Rosanne Welch

The WelchWrite Company
Welchwrite.com/promise

Dedication

To Shirley.

To Douglas and Joseph, who remind me every day about the importance of history and family.

CHAPTER ONE

Saturday mornings, Mary's job was to dust the books in the Holmes' library. Each time, she began by standing in the middle of the room and staring in awe at all the books around her. Mary loved reading, but it was more than that. It was the idea of owning so many books, so much of anything that thrilled her.

Mary wondered how it would feel to own something of her own. Everything she had ever cleaned, cooked or cared for belonged to someone else…even her parents. Even herself. It was 1854 and Mary was a slave on the Holmes' plantation in Louisiana. She was nine years old.

Mary climbed the ladder and took down the largest book in the collection, an old, leather-bound Bible. She poured some linseed oil on her cloth and rubbed the cover gently. The oil moistened the cracks in the binding and shined for a moment then it dried.

Before putting the Bible back on the shelf, Mary opened it. She ran her fingers over the first column trying to recognize the words. She sounded them out slowly as she spoke. 'God saw how good the light was. Then night came and morn-ing fol-lowed'

"The first day..." Buddy completed the sentence from memory as he entered the library, startling Mary.

"You trying to scare me to Jesus, Buddy?" Mary demanded.

"Course not," Buddy answered. "Just bringing coal to start Miss Dorthea's fire." Buddy took his bucket of coal and spread it in the fireplace.

Buddy was a year older than Mary. They had been friends all their lives. "Lucky was me came first and not the mistress."

"Guess I am at that," Mary said gratefully. "Can I help?"

"Naw," Buddy said as he lit the coals. "Less you want to keep reading. Every time I hear it, I put a little to memory. I'm up to the fifth day."

Mary scanned the page until she found the word fifth. Then she read, "'I will make man in my own im-age.'" Mary wrinkled her brow and wondered. "Does that mean God looks like us?"

"Naw, God ain't no slave," Buddy said. "Bible say he's owner of heaven and earth."

"Then he looks like Master Holmes?" Mary asked.

"Shhh!" Buddy whispered suddenly. "Someone's coming."

Mary looked at the ladder across the room. There was no time put the Bible back on the high shelf. She and Buddy ducked behind the sofa instead.

Mary heard her mistress, Miss Dorthea, enter the library, go to the piano and begin her daily music practice.

Mary looked at Buddy. She made a funny face. He made one back. There had been many visitors to the Big House who played the piano very well. Miss Dorthea had not learned much from them.

"How long'll she play?" Buddy whispered. "I got to get back to the field or Mr. Bostwick'll miss me."

"Sometimes she stays all morning," Mary told him.

Buddy's face turned serious. Mary reached out to hold his hand and whispered. "Not always." It didn't seem to help his worrying.

"Dorthea!" The master's voice boomed. Mary heard two sets of footsteps approach.

"Do you have to do that this morning? I'm trying to talk to Robin here, man to man." The master said.

Now it was Mary whose face turned serious. Robin was her Pa. He was tall and sturdy with skin the color of molasses and arms as big as Mary's waist. He was the plantation blacksmith. If the master called him to the library, it meant trouble.

"I need my practice, Tyler," Miss Dorthea said as she continued banging out mismatched notes.

"S'all right, Master," Pa said to Master Holmes. She heard him speak in the quiet, obedient tone he used with the master. It was different from how he spoke to his family or the other slaves. "I accept."

Cautiously, Mary peered from behind the sofa and saw something she had never seen. "Buddy," Mary whispered, "they're shaking hands!"

"Let me see," Buddy asked as he tried to peer around her. But as he looked out, the men were already leaving the room.

What was it all about? Mary wondered. The sound of the piano made it impossible to think.

Finally Miss Dorthea's practice ended and she left. Mary and Buddy returned the Bible to the bookshelf and ran from the room.

CHAPTER TWO

"Ma!" Mary cried, but no one was in the kitchen.

Mary ran outside to the garden, but her mother was not there either. Mary was scared. What if Master Holmes had sold Ma? What if that's why they shook hands? Pa would never let that happen. But how could he stop it? Mary felt like crying. She didn't know what to do. Then, she heard her mother calling for her. "Come here and help me, child."

Mary found her mother, Polly, in Miss Dorthea's bedroom surrounded by the mistress' dresses. Ma was tall, slim and fair skinned with green cat eyes.

"Mama, I was so scared," Mary started to say.

"No time for that when there's work to do," Ma said firmly. "All these dresses got to be folded and packed."

Mary quickly followed her mother's orders as her mother continued, "The master and mistress are taking a train to somewhere called Oregon and we are going with them."

Ma stopped folding for a moment and sat down on the wooden stepstool beside the bed.

"Your Pa says when we get to this Oregon, the Master promised he would free us," Ma nearly whispered.

"Free us?" Mary repeated. "How?"

Her mother drew her near and hugged her. "I barely understand myself. Tonight your Pa will explain."

Ma rose. "I need to get back to the kitchen," she said. "Can you finish this?"

Mary nodded and her mother left the room. Mary was anxious to find Buddy and tell him the news, but she had work to do.

When she finished packing two trunks, Mary went out the back door and into the fields. She saw Buddy working beside his father, Jake, weeding the fields. She ran towards them. Mary was surprised to find her Pa there. He was talking to Jake and another field hand, Uncle Jasper, who was twice her father's age and then some.

She wanted to shout the good news as she ran, but the looks on their faces stopped her.

"What's wrong?" Mary asked Buddy when she reached him.

"Master Holmes is moving and putting us up for sale," Buddy told her sadly.

"But Ma said he promised to free us," Mary insisted.

"He's freeing you and your family, Mary," Jake said. Then he turned to Pa. "And that's only if you live through the journey."

Buddy whispered to Mary, "My Pa says we're escaping. He won't allow no one to sell me or Uncle Jasper away from him like they sold Mama."

"Why can't they come to Oregon with us?" Mary asked her father.

He kneeled down beside her and took her hand. "I wish they could, Mary. I wish they all could. But Master Tyler only promised us."

Mary's excitement now seemed wrong. How could freedom be a good thing without Buddy?

"How can you trust a man who can buy or sell your family at will?" Jake asked Pa.

"He shook hands on it, Jake," Pa said. "He gave his word. To a Southern white man, that's good as gold. Besides, he needs me on this trip. I can read and write and he can't. And for that, he'll give us freedom."

"Yeah, well we ain't got that chance," Jake said. "I have to be sold or run. I'll be gone tonight."

Mary looked at Buddy. He looked back, fear in his eyes. While their fathers continued to argue, Uncle Jasper knelt beside them.

"I don't 'spect children like you know much about freedom," Uncle Jasper said.

"Never met anyone free before," Mary said.

"My great-grandparents was born free in Africa." Uncle Jasper said. "They told my parents all 'bout it and my parents told me. Still, it was all just talk. Before I die, I want to know freedom."

"I want to know it, too," Mary told him.

That night, in their tiny cabin on slave row, Mary and her little brother Turner ate hungrily. Ma had brought leftovers from the Big House, hot sweet potatoes and corn fritters. She added them to greens from her own garden for their dinner.

"Save some for your Pa, children," Ma said. "He should be here soon."

"Will we have corn fritters when we're free?" Mary asked.

"I 'spose we'll have whatever we want then," Ma answered. "That's what free means."

"Then I'll have sugar cubes like they have in the Big House, every night for supper," Turner said with a mouthful of sweet potato.

Suddenly, they heard the high pitched voice of the overseer, Bostwick, shouting outside the cabin.

Ma was staring at the door. Mary had heard other slaves talk about the overseer. He was Miss Dorthea's brother. That's how he kept his job. Mary worried who he was angry with tonight.

Then Mary remembered... Pa was not home yet.

When Ma opened the cabin door, Mary was right behind her. She gasped when she saw Bostwick dragging Jake to a post.

"I'll teach you to steal," Bostwick shouted.

Buddy raced up to his father but Bostwick kicked him away like a dog gone sick in the head. Buddy tried to stumble toward Bostwick again, but someone held him back. Mary squinted her eyes against the dark to see who it was.

"Pa!" Mary shouted.

Her mother quickly clamped a hand around Mary's mouth. "Go back inside. Both of you."

Turner obeyed but Mary could not. She was too scared for her father, for Buddy and for Jake.

Bostwick raised his whip and struck Jake's naked back. Miss Dorthea called to Pa. "You, Robin! Come read for me."

Uncle Jasper grabbed Buddy from behind and held the struggling boy so Pa could walk toward Miss Dorthea.

Pa stood beside the mistress and read from her Bible as Bostwick continued beating Jake. "Slaves must be obedient to their masters in everything."

Polly swallowed hard. Mary tried to hold back her tears.

"They must show complete honesty at all times." Pa continued reading, keeping his eyes from the sight of Jake's bleeding back. "So it is written, so it must be done."

Bostwick yelled over the Bible verses. "This'll teach you to steal food!" He kept beating Jake while Mary and the others could do nothing but watch.

Bostwick finally stopped. He started to lead his sister away from slave row when she turned to Pa. "That's enough, Robin," she said, grabbing the book from his hand.

They disappeared into the darkness. But those around Mary stood still, frozen in their places until the sounds of their footsteps disappeared as well.

Then there was a rush of movement. Pa untied Jake's body and carried it away. Buddy followed.

Mary wanted to follow, too, but Ma held her back. "There's nothing we can do for him now."

CHAPTER THREE

The next morning, Mary was surprised to find Buddy sitting on her father's straw pallet across the room. He was staring out the window, crying.

"Buddy," Mary began. But Ma hushed her.

"Get dressed, Mary," Ma said. "And leave Buddy be."

When Mary and Turner were dressed, Ma took Buddy's hand and they left. Mary took Turner's hand and followed them down the muddy avenue between the cabins.

The only sound she heard this morning was Buddy's muffled sobs. When they reached the end of slave row and turned left instead of right, Mary knew where they were headed. It was the slave cemetery. Her youngest brother was buried there. She saw Pa, Uncle Jasper and some other men standing beside a newly dug grave. Beside it sat Jake's coffin, a simple pine box. They buried him, his head facing to the west and feet to the east, pointing him toward his homeland in Africa.

Mary stood beside Buddy and took his hand. Pa stepped to the front of the grave. "The Lord is my Shepherd, I shall not want." As he recited the rest of the service, the sun finally rose. It was time for the mourners to start their daily work.

After the long day, they gathered in Jake's cabin to remember him. Mary and Ma brought some hoecake they had made. Uncle Jasper played Jake's favorite songs on his fiddle.

Mary watched her brother Turner dance with the other young children as she had danced many times before. But now she didn't feel like dancing. Mary went to sit beside Buddy who was holding a piece of cake in his hand but not eating.

"They caught him with a bag of pecans from the storehouse," Buddy told her. "He took it in case we didn't find enough food on the way North." Buddy threw his hoecake across the room. Some of the younger children made a game of it, gathering the crumbs and stuffing them into their mouths.

"I'm sorry, Buddy," Mary said to her friend. She saw now that he was shivering. "Maybe Pa could ask Master Holmes to let you come with us now."

"Ain't coming with you," Buddy said quietly. "Gonna run away with Jasper."

Mary noticed he didn't call him Uncle Jasper the way she did. It was as if Buddy had suddenly become a man like her father. Mary didn't know what to say. She put her arm over his shoulder.

Buddy asked Mary to step outside.

"Your Pa won't help me, Mary," he whispered. "He doesn't think Jasper and I can make it alone. And we can't. Not without you write us a pass."

"Oh, Buddy," Mary said. "I can't. Pa told me never to write what white folks might see. They'd do me the way..."

"The way they did my Pa?" Buddy said bitterly. "You'll be long gone to Oregon before I ever get caught. No one will know. Please Mary."

Buddy stared into her eyes so deep she thought he could see down to her toes. Then he took her hands.

Finally, she whispered, "I'll do it."

"Thank you, Mary," Buddy said. Instead of releasing her hands, he pulled her close and kissed her on the cheek. Then he ran off into the darkness. Mary stood motionless, wondering what that kiss meant, but she never had the chance to ask him. A week later, Buddy was gone.

At night, Mary prayed Buddy would make it North, even though she missed him. By day she was caught up in the preparations for the trip to Oregon -- and the slave auction.

When the day of the auction arrived, the plantation was filled with men inspecting the slaves who were for sale. Mary walked among the men, keeping their lemonade glasses filled and listening to Bostwick describe her friends. "This boy can tote two bails at a time. And Carrie over here's got ten good years of birthing left in her."

Pa sat beside Master Holmes at a nearby table. The master didn't want the other farmers to know he couldn't read. So Pa held the bills of sale, reading them when no one was looking. If the words on the paper matched what the farmer had said, he'd pass the papers to the master with his right hand. If they didn't, he'd use his left. It was a trick he and the master had used for years.

"Eight hundred?" Master Holmes argued with someone Mary didn't recognize. "Why that boy's been corn fed all his life. You can't do more than eight hundred, you might as well not've come."

Mary looked up and saw that they were talking about Thaddeus, a field hand who lived with his wife next door to Mary's family. Now she would never see him again. She felt bad knowing she was on her way to freedom while he wasn't.

"Nine," another farmer offered.

"Sold," Master Holmes answered quickly.

Thaddeus looked back and forth between the two white men. He took the hand of the woman standing next to him and spoke. "This my wife, Mr. Sir. You need a good breeder?" But no one listened to him.

As the man went off to write out his offer, Thaddeus began to cry.

Mary walked back to the house for more lemonade and another tray of cookies. No one had asked her for more, but she wanted to get as far away from Thaddeus' pain as she could.

That night in their cabin, Mary sat on her straw pallet holding a corn husk doll. She had found it outside their cabin the morning after Buddy and Uncle Jasper left. It had been sitting beside Uncle Jasper's fiddle. Mary named the doll Sadie.

Turner was playing the fiddle now, practicing the same two songs over and over again. Suddenly, he stopped. In the split second before Mary could ask why, the door slammed open. Bostwick stormed into the cabin.

"I got you now," Bostwick said as he hit Pa across the face. The blow was so hard it knocked him down beside Mary. She wanted to hug Pa in fear, or run to some place where Bostwick wouldn't see her. But she couldn't move.

"I don't know what you talking about, Mr. Bostwick," Pa said. He made no move to rise.

Bostwick tossed a crumpled piece of paper on the floor beside Pa. "That," Bostwick said. "That'll keep you from Oregon."

Pa took the piece of paper and unfolded it. Before he could react to it, Mary realized what it was…the travel pass she'd written for Buddy.

"Patrollers brought it over today," Bostwick said. "Dragged two dead Negroes outta the river this morning. Found this on the young one."

Slowly, her father rose. "I didn't write this, Mr. Bostwick, my word," he said.

"Your word?" Bostwick shouted. "Your word means nothing to me, boy. I'm not stupid like Tyler. You can't fool me." Bostwick struck out again, catching Pa on the shoulder and spinning him into the wall.

Mary closed her eyes. She could hear sounds as the beating continued, but she couldn't bear to look. She worried that Bostwick would take her father outside like he did Jake.

"Brother-in-law thinks you'll be helpful on the trail. We'll see what he says after I show him this," Bostwick ranted as he left.

The family stood still until a neighbor finally poked his head in the door. "He gone."

Ma ran to her husband and helped him to his pallet. "Mary, run fetch me some water!"

Mary wanted to tell her father she was sorry that she had caused this trouble, but she was afraid to tell the truth. She walked to his pallet and stared as her mother stripped off his clothes and studied his wounds.

"I said run, child!" Ma yelled. So Mary ran.

CHAPTER FOUR

As the train bumped along the tracks, Mary hugged her doll, Sadie, to her. She shifted her position for the hundredth time, trying to get comfortable. She had lost track of how long her family had been cramped in the semi-darkness of the windowless boxcar. She was just happy the master had allowed them to go after Bostwick showed him the note. The master knew her father's handwriting and saw that it wasn't his. No one had ever seen Mary write.

Mary's parents talked quietly as they stood near the door. Turner was asleep on top of Miss Dorthea's piano. Mary, however, sat on a pile of wooden crates. Every time she moved, prickly splinters worked their way through her clothing.

"How much longer, Ma?" Mary asked.

"I don't know, Mary," Ma answered. "I've never been on a train before."

"Are we still on Holmes' land?" Mary asked her father.

"I don't think so, Mary," he answered. "They say the Oregon Trail starts in a place called Independence, Missouri. I don't know how far off that is from Holmes'."

"Can I have some more cornbread?" Mary asked.

"Why didn't Master Holmes tell us how long this trip would be?" Ma whispered to Pa. "I can't give her all of it. I don't know when I'll be able to make more."

"That's okay, Ma," Mary said. "I'm not really hungry."

Pa smiled at Mary. Then he turned to his wife. Mary couldn't make out what he said. But when he was finished, Ma reached into the canvas sack sitting by her feet. She passed Mary half a piece of cornbread wrapped in a rag.

"Eat slowly," Ma reminded her.

Mary unwrapped the cornbread. She took comfort in the familiar taste of Ma's cooking. But it also reminded her of the last time she had wrapped food in a rag. It had been for Buddy.

Mary had smuggled several pieces of cornbread out of the big house for him. She wanted to smile when she remembered the sight of Buddy stuffing all those pieces into his pockets. But she didn't because she knew Buddy never had the chance to eat them.

"I miss Buddy," she whispered to Sadie.

After eating her cornbread, Mary fell asleep against the wall of the boxcar.

She didn't wake until the great doors were shoved open. Ma and Pa were the first to climb out.

Mary struggled to adjust her eyes to the bright light. At first, all she could see was dust. Then she saw men starting to drag crates off the boxcar. There were many voices outside, some speaking languages she had never heard.

"Come along now, girl," a tall man said loudly. "You're in the way."

Mary climbed down from her tower of crates and Pa helped her out of the boxcar. Turner stood beside him, rubbing his eyes and calling for something to eat.

"Not now, boy," Master Holmes said. "We've got work to do. You -- Polly." He pointed at Ma. "Miss Dorthea's resting at the hotel. Go see to her."

Ma grabbed Mary's hand and they walked down the railroad platform. As they passed the end of the train, they saw a row of buildings crammed together across the street. Ma stopped walking.

"Ma," Mary asked, gently tugging her mother's arm. "What kind of plantation is this?"

"I don't know, child," Ma said quietly. She stared from building to building, from person to person. That's when Mary noticed a few other people in the crowd who looked like them. A dark-skinned woman was dumping a pail of dirty water into the muddy street. They walked over to her.

"Ma'am?" Ma asked. "I wonder, could you tell me which is the hotel? My mistress is there and I, I –"

"No bother, honey," the older woman said. "It's right over there. Tallest place in town." She pointed to a four story clapboard building.

"Thank you kindly," Ma said as they turned to go.

"We're going on the Oregon Trail and when we get there, we'll be free." Mary couldn't help blurting out her news before they left.

"'Been free since Old Master died back in '42, nigh on twelve years now," the woman said. "Name's Carolina."

"I'm Polly and this is my daughter, Mary," Ma said.

"Pleased to meet you," Carolina said. Then she knelt down, eye-to-eye with Mary. "It's quite a blessing to know your Mama, young girl. Never knew mine."

As they headed toward the hotel, Mary looked back to wave at Carolina, but the older woman was busy with her work again.

When they reached the hotel, Mary marveled at how large the building was. That night, her mind was so full of new sights she barely slept.

The next morning, Mary returned to the busy street. She toted boxes of perfume bottles, vases and books to and from the wagons as Miss Dorthea decided where her special things best fit.

Everything from the giant piano to the tiniest box had to be loaded onto the two wagons Master Holmes had purchased for the trip. They were parked at the edge of town, already lined up among 150 other wagons. There seemed to be wagons as far as Mary could see. Cattle were tied to the back of many of them, placidly chewing their cud. Dogs ran freely around their owners, including Master Holmes' two ugly bloodhounds.

When Mary walked toward the wagon, the dogs ran to her, barking and snapping. Mary had always avoided them on the plantation. She'd seen Bostwick send them to chase down runaways too many times. Mary was so frightened when the dogs came at her that she wanted to run back to the hotel, but Master Holmes had already seen her. "Down, boys!" He shouted at the dogs. "Down!"

The dogs ran back to their master, but Mary didn't feel safe until she reached her father's side.

"All right Master Holmes," Pa said. "I got everything lashed and secured inside the supply wagon. We're almost ready to go."

"Tyler, I want you to see that my piano and my good china is tied down tight," Miss Dorthea said. "Twenty-two hundred miles is a long way." She was seated at the front of the wagon, wearing her veiled bonnet to shield her from the sun.

"Didn't the boy just tell me that, Dorthea?" Master Holmes answered her. "'Sides, I don't know why I 'lowed you to bring that mess in the first place. Better to 'low space for a plow or more seed bags. Ain't got no use for a piano. Much less for china."

"Fine dining and gracious living is appropriate anywhere civilized men and women go," Miss Dorthea snapped. "Without these things we might slide back into your family's common ways." Then she corrected his grammar to show her better breeding when she added, "Be-sides, we appear to be the only respectable people heading to Oregon."

Mary's eyes followed Miss Dorthea's as the mistress glanced at the nearby wagons and their owners. Most of them were suntanned farmers with children in tow, some wearing clothes in worse condition than Mary's.

"Why some of these people don't even own slaves. Best keep to ourselves until we find our own kind," Miss Dorthea said.

Bostwick rode up on his horse. Dorthea tried to draw him into the conversation. "Isn't that right, brother?" she asked.

Master Holmes finished instructing Pa before he said hello to his brother-in-law. "Robin, I want you to drive the supply wagon. I'll handle the family wagon. Bostwick here'll ride behind and keep a look out."

"I'm not trusting all our supplies to him," Bostwick said as he spat a glob of chewing tobacco out of his mouth. "I plan to drive the supply wagon."

The two white men stared at each other. Standing beside her father, Mary squeezed his hand warmly. It was all she knew to do to remind him she was on his side.

Master Holmes finally gave in. "You drive it," he said to Bostwick. "Robin'll walk with the rest of them."

When Master Holmes and Bostwick walked away, Mary whispered to her father, "I don't mind walking, Pa. Buddy was going to walk to freedom. He just never got the chance."

Pa reached down and hugged her. "You're my sunshine, Mary. Always trying to think bright."

Pleased by his praise, Mary returned to packing the final items. She picked up Miss Dorthea's box and walked with it to the wagon.

"No! No!" Mary cried as the dogs ran to her again. This time, Master Holmes wasn't around to stop them.

CHAPTER FIVE

"No, no!" Pa yelled, but the dogs weren't trained to listen to his voice.

One of the dogs jumped up and planted his front paws on Mary's shoulders, knocking her down. Miss Dorthea's box flew from Mary's hands. It landed upside down in the mud surrounding a nearby watering trough.

Pa pulled the dog off before it could bite Mary. Miss Dorthea jumped off her seat in the wagon and came running.

"What's happened?" Miss Dorthea screamed. She took in the situation quickly: Mary on the ground, her father holding the dog back and the box lying in the road. Miss Dorthea ran to the box and opened it.

"My mother's Bible!" Miss Dorthea shouted. "You stupid girl! You've nearly ruined it!" Mary saw that some of the mud had soaked into the pages of the old book.

Miss Dorthea started crying before Mary could apologize. Ma ran over to help her up.

"Mary! Are you all right?" Ma asked.

Bostwick stormed over to Mary and raised his hand. Mary closed her eyes, anticipating the sting of his slap. But instead she heard her mother cry, "No!"

"You talking back to me?" Bostwick demanded.

Mary opened her eyes to see her mother standing between her and the overseer. People in other wagons were staring, unsure of what to do.

"You know what happened last time you flapped your lip to me, don't you girl?" Bostwick said in the low, menacing voice he used before he took the whip to someone.

"You can do what you like to me," Ma said slowly. "But not my young `uns. Not no more."

"I'm sorry," Mary blurted out, trying to draw his attention. "I'm sorry, Miss Dorthea, but them dogs --"

"Shut up girl!" Bostwick said.

"Please don't hit Polly, sir," Pa asked. "Or my daughter. It was an accident."

Bostwick spoke snidely to Ma. "I'll never know why my brother-in-law insists on bothering with y'all --"

"Because they listen better than you do," Master Holmes said as he returned to the wagon. "I told you never to hit her again," he said pointing to Mary's mother. "She ain't borne no children since the last beating. I could have had six or more field hands out of her."

As the two stood facing each other again, another white man rode up. He didn't look or sound like any of the men Mary knew. He dressed like the ministers who came to dine at the big house, all in black with a crisp, white shirt.

"Excuse me, gentlemen," the man said. Mary noticed that he smiled at all the men present as he spoke, even her father. "I am Charles McPhedren. I am leading this wagon train and I was told one of thee could read and write."

When no one else answered, Pa said, "That would be me, sir."

Mr. McPhedren turned to him. "I am in need of someone to assist in keeping up the entries in the travel log and doing some simple arithmetic, helping to calculate our mileage, distance traveled per day and the like. Would thee be willing to ride at the front of the wagons with me and do so?"

Pa looked to Master Holmes, who seemed to be weighing the idea.

Bostwick stepped in to the conversation. "Just a minute," he said. "I'm Bostwick, this here's Tyler Holmes and his wife, my sister, Dorthea."

Mr. McPhedren tipped his hat to Miss Dorthea.

Bostwick continued, "This here's a slave on the Holmes' plantation. He and them others take orders from me."

"Or me," Master Holmes reminded Bostwick. "I don't see no harm in Robin here helping out."

"It is settled then," Mr. McPhedren said to Master Holmes. "Might I prevail on thy good faith a second time? My wife's in the family way and requires someone to drive our wagon for us." He glanced from Ma to Miss Dorthea. "Might one of thee kind ladies be free for that chore?"

Miss Dorthea was insulted to be considered in the same breath as her maid. "I am the only lady here."

"Begging thy pardon, Mrs. Holmes," Mr. McPhedren said politely. "We are Quakers. We believe all are created equal in God's eyes."

"Fine," Master Holmes said quickly, "Robin and Polly can help you. As long as they all return to our wagon whenever we need them and they don't fall behind in their work."

As the grown-ups around her discussed the details of this new arrangement, Mary wondered about Mr. McPhedren. Mary had never heard of Quakers. What she had heard of God came mostly from Miss Dorthea. She had held church in slave row every Sunday morning.

The mistress had taught Mary that God meant for whites to be masters, and it was a sin to disobey Him. Mary was confused. Whose God was right? Miss Dorothea's or Mr. McPhedren's?

CHAPTER SIX

"Never forget that everyone, whether slave or free man, will be rewarded by the Lord for whatever work he has done well." As she sat beside her mother on the front seat of the McPhedren's wagon, Mary listened to Miss Alice read from her Bible. The young woman was lying on a pile of blankets on the floor of the wagon with small boxes tied to the sides of the wagon around her.

The wagon train had been traveling for several weeks and Mary was taking a break from walking. Still, she didn't mind the walking. Her memories of Buddy helped. So did the fact that all the other children on the trip were walking, too. It was the first time Mary and Turner had been treated no differently than the white children in their world.

Mary enjoyed hearing Miss Alice read from her Bible. The kind Quaker woman was younger than Miss Dorthea, even younger than Ma. And she was going to have a baby. Soon. "And those of you who are employers of slaves, treat your slaves in the same spirit," Miss Alice read.

Mary had never heard these words in all the Sundays of Miss Dorthea's Bible readings.

"Do without threats and never forget that they and you have the same Master in heaven and there is no favoritism in Him," Miss Alice finished.

"Is that truly in there, Miss Alice? It don't sound like no Bible I ever was read," Mary blurted the words out before she knew it. "I'm sorry, ma'am," She hurriedly added. "I didn't mean to--"

"No fear child," Miss Alice hushed her. "These are the words of the Lord, thy God."

"Are you cold, Miss Alice?" Ma asked.

"No more than the others on this journey, Polly, but I thank thee for thy concern," Miss Alice answered.

Ma took off the small quilt she was using as a shawl and handed it to Mary. "Put this around Miss Alice's feet. They be the coldest as her time get closer."

Mary crawled through the McPhedren's meager possessions, mostly tools and food. Then she wrapped the quilt around Miss Alice.

"Did thy mother make this, Mary?" Miss Alice asked. "It's beautiful."

"Thank you, Miss Alice," Ma said quietly.

"Did thee make it for thy obedient daughter?" Miss Alice asked.

Ma was silent.

"Or young Turner?" Miss Alice spoke louder. She must have thought Ma couldn't hear her. "Or have thee another left behind?"

Mary started to tell Miss Alice about her other brother, but her mother quickly interrupted. "He was just as perfect as he could be," Ma said quietly,"but had no breath in him. Bostwick knocked it out when he beat me."

"I am sorry," Miss Alice said.

"It's all right, Miss Alice," Ma said. "You didn't know."

Mary was uncomfortable in the silence that followed. She moved toward the front of the wagon, hoping to jump down and start walking again, to be alone with her thoughts.

Miss Alice's words held her back. She was reading from the Bible again. "'There is an appointed time for' -- Oh, my eyes can't find the words in this light. I wish my Charlie was here to read these words of comfort to thee, Polly."

"I can read it for you," Mary offered. Ma shot her a look. Then she remembered her father's warnings about hiding your knowledge from whites. But it was too late to take back.

"Then please, for me, would thee read this passage to thy mother?" Miss Alice held out the Bible again, no sign of reproach in her voice. "I believe it will give comfort in the memory of the child she lost."

Reassured, Mary took the Bible and began reading aloud where Miss Alice pointed, sounding out the difficult words. "'There is an ap-pointed time for every-thing and a time for every af-fair under the heavens. A time to be born and a time to die. A time to plant and a time to up-root the plant. A time to hurt and a time to heal.'"

At nightfall, the wagons stopped at a giant rock which had many names carved around its base. Mr. McPhedren gathered the many travelers around the rock and told them it was called The Great Register.

"Do you see all of the names? Travelers on this route have left their mark here, as a sign to those who come behind them, that they made it this far. Now it is our turn." He demonstrated by carving his name and Miss Alice's on the rock.

Other travelers carved their family names, too.

Mary saw Miss Dorthea nudge her husband. "Make Robin put our names up."

"Go on, Robin," Master Holmes said as he handed Pa his knife.

When he finished carving Holmes on the rock, Mary asked Pa, "Can't we put our names up too?"

"Don't be silly, child," Miss Dorthea said. "You belong to us. You're Holmes, too."

Disappointed, Mary went back to the wagon.

That evening Mary and her family made dinner for the master and mistress and saw to the animals and their needs. Then Pa asked Mary to take a walk with him. They walked back to the Great Register, far enough away from the wagons that no one could overhear them.

"Mary," Pa said in the voice she knew meant trouble."Did you write Buddy's travel pass?"

Mary had never lied to her father before, yet many lies suddenly jumped to her mind. "No," she said.

"We both know the handwriting on that travel pass wasn't mine," Pa scolded her.

"I'm sorry, Pa. I never wanted anyone to get hurt. Especially not you. I just wanted to help Buddy," Mary confessed.

Her father knelt beside her and dried her tears with the old rag he used as a handkerchief. Then he kissed her cheeks. "It's important for a slave to know when to lie and when to tell the truth. Your life may depend on it. Promise me you'll be careful."

Mary nodded. It was quiet all around them except for the coyotes baying in the distance.

"We all miss him, Mary," Pa said. "But, we might have lost you as well. That pass didn't look real --"

"I know my handwriting isn't proper, but if you teach me--" Mary said.

"If Bostwick finds out," Pa said.

"But he won't, Pa, he won't," Mary said. "And soon, we'll be in Oregon and free of him. Isn't that what you promised?"

"Then let's start tonight," Pa said. He pulled the knife out of his pocket and handed it to Mary. She opened the blade and began to carve her name on the rock.

Pa smiled as he watched her, "Free children," he said. "Ain't been no free children in my family since..." He went quiet again.

"Since now," Mary said. She hugged her father just as the first drops of rain fell for the night.

CHAPTER SEVEN

Two days later, the downpour had not ceased. Mary was soaked to the skin. Walking in the rain, there had been no chance to dry out. Now, she sat in the back of the McPhedren's wagon as it sloshed through the Columbia River. Ma held Miss Alice's hand. Mary steadied the boxes piled around them as the wagon rocked and jolted across the wide expanse.

"Yippee!" Mary cried as the horses' hooves touched land again. They were the first wagon across the river.

She listened as Mr. McPhedren patiently urged the horses to draw the entire wagon out of the waters. He did it with a calm voice and a prayer, techniques Master Holmes had never used.

"Now that we know the river is safe, we will pull aside to assist the others," Mr. McPhedren called back to the women in the wagon.

"Yippee," Miss Alice echoed in her loudest whisper. "Thank thee, Lord, and thank thee, Charles." She turned to Ma. "I hope thy husband and son have as good a crossing."

Once the movement stopped, Mr. McPhedren poked his head through the double layered entrance, trying to shield his wife from the rain. "Take thee thy rest. Polly? Wouldst thou mind if I asked for the assistance of thy child to pass messages to the other wagons?"

"No, sir," Ma answered. "Be about as wet as she can be already, I guess."

Mary tucked Sadie into her rope belt and followed Mr. McPhedren to the shore in time to see her father maneuver the Holmes' wagon up over the bank. He followed the path that Mr. McPhedren had forged. Turner was riding the lead horse, helping to guide it straight. Mary cheered them both on.

Then she saw Master Holmes steer his horses into the rising river. They crossed just as easily until the wagon reached the bank. Instead of rolling over the mud, the wooden wheels sank into it. Master Holmes whipped the horses with the reins.

"Go gentle with them, Friend Holmes!" Mr. McPhedren shouted encouragement, but the strong wind blew his words away.

"Robin!" Master Holmes shouted. Pa was on the riverbank beside her and Mr. McPhedren. "You and Turner get back there and push!"

"The more he mangles the bank, the harder for the others to cross!" Mr. McPhedren warned.

Without being asked, he joined Pa and Turner behind the wheels of the heavy wagon. Their legs sank in the mud around the wheels and they were quickly up to their waists in water. They were soon so covered with mud you couldn't tell there was a white man among them.

"It ain't gonna make it up with this load in it!" Pa shouted to Master Holmes. Then he spoke to Turner. "You and your sister gather some ropes from the nearby wagons. We need enough to reach the trees 'cross the river."

"Ah," Mr. McPhedren said, "we can use the trees for leverage in pulling up the wagon. God's gifts are everywhere."

As she and Turner gathered rope from the nearby wagons, Mary thought about Mr. McPhedren. She was amazed that even buried knee deep in mud he could find his God's help when he needed it.

When the ropes were collected and tied together they formed a pulley from the wagon to the trees. Several men from other wagons crossed the river to help pull, but still the wagon remained trapped.

"Friend Holmes!" Mr. McPhedren shouted to Master Holmes. "We are losing our strength to this folly. Thy wagon is overloaded and must be relieved before we can hope to save it."

"Robin!" Master Holmes shouted back. "Get up here and drive this thing whilst I figure what to dump."

"No!" cried Miss Dorthea from inside the wagon. Her face was framed by the wagon flaps which she had pulled apart to watch the proceedings. Wet curls clung to her forehead.

Pa took control of the horses as Master Holmes ignored his wife and heaved a heavy trunk into the water. Its locks popped open on the rocks and papers scattered in the wind, plastering themselves against the muddy bank around them.

The horses and the men on the ropes pulled again, but no progress was made.

"More!" Mr. McPhedren called from his place on the rope. "'Tis not enough!"

"Turner, help me with this!" Master Holmes called. Turner slid down the bank in an instant. Master Holmes helped him into the bowels of the wagon and pointed. Soon, one of Miss Dorthea's velvet arm chairs was teetering on the edge.

"No!" Miss Dorthea cried again. This time her horror drew her out into the rain. She raced to the bank as the chair landed in the river with a splash.

"More chairs!" Master Holmes yelled back as Turner pushed another one to the edge. Then the master turned back to his wife. "Don't argue with me, Dorthea, something's gotta go!"

"Then let me help!" she begged.

"You couldn't pick any of it!" Master Holmes shouted as he pointed to another trunk. Turner edged it towards him.

"My china!" Miss Dorthea screamed. "Mother's tea set!" She opened the trunk and dug around in the velvet wrapped interior, clutching several things to her. The men on the shore were getting impatient.

"Enough, Dorthea," Master Holmes said, taking her hands. "You can have Oregon or you can have china."

Mary had never seen her mistress cry over anything, but there she stood, up to her ankles in mud, crying over a teacup.

"It's moving, Master Holmes!" Pa shouted from the driver's seat as the weight was lifted.

"Go back to the other wagon," Master Holmes told his wife. She headed up the bank, collecting small, discarded things along the way.

"Help me, child!" Miss Dorthea demanded.

Mary bent down to retrieve the bottom of a butter dish and whatever other pieces she could hold in her apron. Her hands were full as she followed Miss Dorthea. Then she turned to watch as Master Holmes and Mr. McPhedren stood clear of the wheels and they were finally pulled from the mud.

Mary was about to cheer when she saw her doll Sadie sinking into the mud. It had slipped from her belt as Mary collected china. She ran to grab it from under the wagon wheels, but Miss Dorthea pulled her away. "Are you daft, child?" the mistress shouted.

Before Mary could explain, the Holmes' wagon rolled onto the bank and the doll Uncle Jasper had made for Mary was no more.

CHAPTER EIGHT

As the wagons stopped for the day, Mary gathered buffalo chips in her apron to build a fire for her mother to cook the evening meal. She wished she were a boy like Turner. He got to help their father feed the horses and look after the cows. Mary would much rather do that.

"Why do we use animal droppings to start a fire?" Mary asked her mother as she cooked. Mary tried to stand on the opposite side of the smoke which came from the fire. It smelled like the outhouse back on the plantation.

"We never did this back home," Mary said.

"There were trees back home and firewood aplenty. There're no trees on the trail. This'll burn just as well," Ma explained.

Once their work was done, Mary's family sat with the McPhedrens.

Mr. McPhedren blessed the evening meal. "It is important to thank God that we have made it through another day."

"Why?" Mary asked.

"Many before us never made it to Oregon," Mr. McPhedren answered. "The Donner Party was caught in the mountains near about four months by an early winter storm." Mr. McPhedren glanced at her father before he continued. "When the rescue party reached them, no more than half were left alive."

"What happened to them?" Mary asked.

"Just you never mind," Pa said.

"Some boys round the community fire say they ate each other," Turner said excitedly. Mary couldn't believe that, but she never knew her brother to be a liar.

Mr. McPhedren dismissed the tale. "There are all sorts of stories about how they survived. Only the Lord knows the truth."

Pa said. "Sometimes a man must do what he has to to survive."

"I pray that won't happen to us," Mr. McPhedren said.

After supper, Pa helped her with her reading and writing. They sat in the McPhedren's wagon so no one else would see them.

Mary read the line her father pointed out in the Bible. "Masters, make sure your slaves are given what is upright and fair, knowing that you too have a Master in Heaven."

"Now," Pa said, "copy it down."

Mary wrote on the back pages of Mr. McPhedren's travel log. Mary's father warned her not to show the book to anyone else.

"When you have knowledge," Pa continued, "You're either feared or coveted by your master. Some will be afraid you'll use it to run off. Others will keep you by their side and use what you know, keeping you from freedom."

44

"Aren't we getting free 'cause Master Tyler needs your help?" Mary asked.

"Well yes, but `til we get to Oregon and are free," Pa said, "we must be careful." Mary continued writing until her mother called them to bed down for the night.

The next morning, Mary milked the cow and hung the bucket of cream under the wagon. It would churn while they traveled and become butter by sundown. Then she spent the rest of the day walking beside her father and Mr. McPhedren as they rode at the front of the wagon train. Mary liked being near her father.

"Mr. McPhedren..." Pa started to ask.

Mr. McPhedren said, "No Mister is needed. Thee and I are friends."

"It will be hard," Pa responded, "I've always called white men Master. I was raised with my first master's son, Master William. He was the one who taught me to read and write. Even though it was forbidden, he wanted me to know what he knew." He paused for a moment and then continued. "When Master William's father found out, he sold me to Master Holmes."

"If Master Holmes hadn't bought you," Mary said to her father, "then you wouldn't have met Ma."

Pa smiled. "That's true. I love your Ma, but I wish my Ma and Pa could be with us as well."

Mary had never seen her grandparents. Her father rarely spoke of them.

Mary could not imagine her family ever separated. Although they were slaves, they had been lucky. Master Holmes had kept them together, kept them a family.

"If it's thy Lord's will, thee will be together again some day," Mr. McPhedren said.

Mary wondered why God would allow people who loved each other to be separated. Maybe it wasn't God who decided. Miss Dorthea always said God meant for white men to match and breed slaves. Mary didn't believe that. The more she learned, the more she began to think the things Miss Dorthea said might not be true.

"Well then," Mr. McPhedren continued, "Thee must needs get used to calling me by my given name. Oregon is a territory which does not support slavery. Thee will not have a man as thy master ever again. The Lord will by thy only master."

"I reckon you're right...Friend Charlie." Both men laughed as Pa called Mr. McPhedren by his first name.

CHAPTER NINE

Later that night, Mary and her mother served the Holmes their evening meal, beans soaked in molasses and water with sliced potato. Ma dished it into small metal bowls from the slave quarters because all of Miss Dorthea's fine china had broken. Things were different now, out on the trail. Maybe that is what freedom promised, Mary thought, everyone eating off the same plate.

"What kind of stew is this?" Master Holmes asked. He took another bite and tossed his spoon back into the bowl.

Miss Dorthea tasted it and scowled. She snapped at Ma. "Polly, how could you serve us this mess? There's no meat in it. Where are the biscuits?"

Ma looked to Bostwick, who continued eating. "There's no meat left," she said quietly. "And little flour for biscuits."

"What about our supplies, the dried beef, the salt pork?" Master Holmes demanded.

"That's gone, too." Again, Ma glanced at Bostwick, but Mary noticed he would not meet her eye. "We ran out of those long ago. I told Mister Bostwick so myself."

"We have over twenty-five dollars saved up to buy supplies. What happened?" Master Holmes asked.

"I got cheated at the trading post," Bostwick finally admitted.

Master Holmes turned on Bostwick with a rage that Mary had never seen directed towards anyone but a slave. "How could that happen? I sent Robin with you to cipher the money!"

"Maybe that slave of yours isn't as smart as you think," Bostwick lied.

Pa defended himself. "Mister Bostwick had me stand outside the door. Said he didn't need my help."

"Bostwick! How could you?" Master Holmes demanded.

Bostwick was silent for a while. This time, Mary thought, the mistress could not save him from Master Holmes' wrath. Finally he said, "I don't need a Negro looking over my shoulder."

"Apparently you do," Master Holmes snapped. Bostwick looked down into his stew.

Ma and Pa went to see to their work. They knew better than to be around when the master was mad.

"Mary, bring the butter from the wagon hitch," Ma suggested. As Mary struggled to untie the heavy bucket, Master Holmes continued arguing with Bostwick.

"There's another thousand miles to go before we reach the Oregon coast. How are we supposed to live with little food and no money?" Master Holmes demanded.

Miss Dorthea exchanged a look with her brother and gave her advice. "We can eat what's left. The slaves can find their own food."

Master Holmes snorted. "Makes no sense to starve the only valuable property we have left. Especially after losing everything else on the trail. We'll need them in Oregon."

"I heard some men talking," Bostwick said. Master Holmes glared at him, but Bostwick continued. "They say Hudspith Cutoff is up ahead. If we take that turn off, we can head to California. It's closer than Oregon, and in California, they got gold." Bostwick's eyes gleamed.

Miss Dorthea seemed to share his excitement. "Gold...?"

Tyler hushed them both. "I'm a farmer, not a miner. I'm not going to California."

"Well, I am," Bostwick said. "A man can get rich mining for gold. Then I won't have to work for anyone."

"Good, go on then," Master Holmes snapped back.

"Will you be safe on that trail?" Miss Dorthea cried.

Bostwick tried to comfort her. "There are others going. With a horse and a pitch tent, I should do all right." Bostwick looked cautiously at Master Holmes. "But," he continued, "instead of taking my last pay, I'll take my portion of the supplies."

49

Master Holmes exploded, "We're low because of you!"

Miss Dorthea pleaded, "But Tyler, he can't go off by himself without any food. He'll starve."

"Well," Master Holmes finally said, "If it'll help me be rid of you, then so be it."

It was hard for Mary to sleep that night. Like many on the trail, Mary and her family slept under the wagons for shelter and warmth. It was not the cold that kept Mary awake, it was her parents' whispers.

"You hear how he talks about us?" Ma worried. "It's as if he plans for us to be his slaves forever."

Pa tried to calm her. "Don't worry, Polly. Master Holmes made us a promise of freedom, and I believe him."

CHAPTER TEN

The next day, after only a few hours on the trail, Mr. McPhedren stopped the wagons and ordered everyone to circle. He proudly announced they had made it to South Pass, the halfway point to Oregon. They would make camp and celebrate that evening.

At the McPhedren's wagon, Mary built a fire for Miss Alice.

"That is fine," said Miss Alice, with a weak smile on her face. "Go and join the others at the celebration fire. I thank thee for thy kindness." She tucked herself tightly in her blankets and nodded off to sleep.

Mary joined her family and the others who were sharing food and drink in front of a fire much bigger than Miss Alice's. In fact, it was taller than Mary.

Mary was surprised to see her master and mistress at the celebration. It was the first community gathering they had attended. Mary turned to Pa and said, "I thought they weren't coming because they didn't have food to share."

"Is that true, Friend Robin?" Mr. McPhedren asked. Pa nodded his head.

"Then the Lord would have us offer them some of ours," Mr. McPhedren continued. He walked over to where the Holmes were sitting.

His offer of food threw Miss Dorthea into a rage. "I told you we shouldn't have come, Tyler. Imagine being insulted by such common people." She turned to Mr. McPhedren and continued, "Why should we take charity from you? Your kind mixes with Negroes. You're no better than a servant."

"We are all servants of God," Mr. McPhedren replied.

Miss Dorthea shouted, "I know the Good Book. I live by it. How dare you quote me scripture. Miss Dorthea stormed back to the wagon.

"The trip's been hard on her," Master Holmes said in apology. Then he reluctantly followed his wife.

Mr. McPhedren shook his head. "We must pray for them," he told Mary.

"Why?" Mary asked. She was sure Miss Dorthea never prayed for her.

"We must pray for those who are lost and need to find their way," Mr. McPhedren said.

A German man with a funny accent yelled to Turner. "Can ya play `Turkey in the Straw', son?"

For the most part, the other travelers on the wagon train were from all over - Northern cities, Southern farms, even people from foreign lands. Though they spoke different languages, music was a language they all understood.

Turner picked up Uncle Jasper's fiddle, which he had carried throughout the trip in a burlap sack slung over his shoulder.

"See, Mary," Turner said with pride, "other people want to hear me play."

After playing the two songs Uncle Jasper had taught him, the crowd called for more.

"What should I do, Pa?" Turner asked.

"Perhaps you should play the first song again," Pa said. As Turner started to repeat the song, Pa headed to the Holmes' wagon.

"Where are you going, Pa?" Mary asked.

"To check on the master and mistress," he said.

"Can I come with you?" Mary asked.

They walked toward the wagons as the crowd laughed, hollered, and danced, enjoying the company too much to care about Turner's limited repertoire.

As Mary and her father approached the wagon, they could see that Miss Dorthea was still angry. Master Holmes seemed happy for their interruption.

"I want my own fire," Miss Dorthea demanded of her husband.

"I told you, Dorthea," he said, "there's nothing left to burn."

Pa added, "That's right, Miss Dorthea, all the chips went into the community fire."

"I want my own fire, like Alice McPhedren has," Miss Dorthea pouted.

"But she's in the family way," Mary blurted out, "and can't leave her wagon."

"Shut up, girl," Miss Dorthea said angerly. "I want a real fire. I want a wood fire."

"We haven't had a wood fire since we left Missouri," Pa reminded her.

Master Tyler looked into the wagon and smiled. "I bet the wood from this piano would burn just fine."

"Not my piano!" As Miss Dorthea wailed in horror, Master Holmes picked up an ax and swung it at the piano. Wood scattered and wires burst. Mary looked at Pa, who was trying hard not to laugh.

CHAPTER ELEVEN

The weather turned colder. Mary noticed that when the horses whinnied, warm air came out of their nostrils like mist. The days were grey and often the clouds let loose handfuls of white flakes from the sky. Mary had never seen snow before. Mr. McPhedren said this was a sign that winter was coming and they must hurry. Mary rode in the McPhedren's wagon to keep Miss Alice company now that her time was near.

"Whoa! Halt the wagons!" Mr. McPhedren called. His command echoed back as each man repeated the order. The wagons came to a halt at a frozen lake which stretched to the horizon. In the middle of the lake, several wagons had broken through the ice. The wagon wheels stuck up out of the frozen water.

Mr. McPhedren shook his head sadly. He dismounted from his horse and spoke to those gathered at the edge of the lake. "We will pull them from the water. Even in this wilderness, these men deserve a proper burial."

"What a waste of time," Miss Dorthea complained. "We should continue so we don't get stuck in the mountains during a storm."

"Dorthea, it's only Christian that we bury them." Master Holmes grabbed a shovel off of his wagon and went to join the other men.

They worked in shifts over several days, taking turns between removing the bodies, digging graves, and sleeping. The women prepared food and kept hot coffee on the fire. One day, while Mary was preparing Miss Dorthea's breakfast, Pa approached. "I'm lookin' to speak with Master Holmes, ma'am."

"Tyler's asleep. He's worn himself out with this nonsense. I hope you're near done," Miss Dorthea said.

"Yes, ma'am," Pa said. "I believe we found the last of them. But I really need to speak to Master Holmes."

"Anything you have to say to him, you can say to me," Miss Dorthea snapped.

Pa hesitated.

"Tell me!" Miss Dorthea ordered.

"I found this around the neck of one of the men." Pa handed Miss Dorthea a silver locket. She recognized the jewelry instantly.

Mary recognized it, too. It had been her job to polish the locket once a month back on the plantation. It had belonged to Miss Dorthea's mother.

"No! No! I gave this to Bostwick. He can't be...he can't..." Miss Dorthea started to cry.

"Mr. Charlie says he'll give a service first thing tomorrow mornin'." Pa said. "And I'll dig the grave myself."

"I won't leave my Bostwick here. Not in the middle of nowhere. I won't leave him alone." Miss Dorthea fell to the ground. In her grief, she pounded her fists on the frozen dirt.

"But he's not alone, Miss Dorthea," Mary said. "He's with God." But Miss Dorthea could not hear Mary over her own sobs.

"Mary, Mary, come quick!" Ma called from the McPhedren's wagon. "I need your help." Mary looked to her Pa who motioned for her to leave.

Mary ran from the Holmes' wagon towards the McPhedren's. Mary's mother told her to collect two buckets of water. Mary went to where the men had cut a hole in the ice and scooped out the water. She brought it back to the wagon, where Miss Alice was breathing heavily and could not catch her breath. Mary's mother talked calmly to her and held her hand.

"Mary, set that water to boil and soak these rags in it." Mary did as she was told. Ma had helped many women on the plantation give birth. Unless a baby was real sick, and even then, often the master would not call a doctor from town.

Finally, Miss Alice let out a loud cry and their baby was born. Mary handed the baby to Mr. McPhedren. He said they would name him after David, who conquered Goliath in the Bible.

"Our son will overcome great things and serve his God well," Mr. McPhedren said. He stroked Miss Alice's cheek and kissed the baby on the forehead.

Miss Alice could not speak. She simply smiled and closed her eyes. Tears ran down her face. Mary washed David in the rags she had soaked in hot water. Soon he was clean and white. Mary had never before seen a child so pale.

"It's just his coloring, Mary. Just as we come in all shades of brown, black and tan, baby David is a lighter shade of white than his mother or father. A few weeks in the sun and he'll look right fine," Ma said.

But her mother was wrong, he stayed pale. No matter what she did, Miss Alice could not get the baby to eat.

"What is wrong, Polly," Miss Alice asked, worried.

"I don't know," Ma worried.

After two days of taking neither milk from Miss Alice nor corn which Mary had mashed and mixed with cow's milk, baby David stopped crying.

"My baby!" Miss Alice screamed. "My baby won't wake!"

Ma tried her best to help. But despite her efforts, baby David died.

They stopped the wagons to bury him. Mr. McPhedren marked the headstone with two sticks which he had whittled and bound together into a cross. He tried to comfort Miss Alice.

"It is God's will," he said.

"How can God take a baby from its mother?" Mary protested. "It is not right!"

Miss Alice cried softly. Ma cradled Miss Alice in her arms. Mary had not cried when they buried Mr. Bostwick. But the next morning, when Mary woke, her pillow was wet with tears.

CHAPTER TWELVE

As they crossed the valley, the land turned green and lush instead of brown. Now, they were surrounded by pine trees, grassy fields and mountains capped with white.

"Does thou see Fort Vancouver, that is the end of the trail," Mr. McPhedren said to Mary.

Mary looked out from the wagon flaps at the tall wooden fort in the distance.

"Ain't no one around, not a town or nothing," Mary said.

"Oregon is a new territory, Mary," Mr. McPhedren replied. "There are very few people who live here."

"But more arrive every day," Pa said. He took off his hat and wiped the sweat from his face. "Been a long trip, but we made it." He put his arm around Mary and gave her a squeeze.

"Yippee!" Mary cried. "Does this mean we free, Pa?" Mary asked.

Pa quieted her. "Not yet, Sunshine, first we have to help Master Holmes and Miss Dorthea build their farm."

Mr. McPhedren smiled. "We will build ours near thee. In wilds such as this, it is important to have good neighbors."

"Amen to that," Pa said.

"Amen, indeed," said Mr. McPhedren.

The Holmes were given sixty acres of land by the government for settling in the territory. As Master Holmes and Pa walked the property, Master Holmes pointed out where the buildings would go.

"I want the barn over here, down wind of the house. And the well, dig it near the cooking area. We can set up an outhouse yonder near the stream. That area there will be for planting." Master Holmes instructed while Pa made notes on a piece of paper.

In the following months, Mary's family readied the land for planting. They cleared trees, turned the earth and planted seeds. Once that was done, Master Holmes, Pa and Turner laid logs atop one another to build the house and barn. They sealed them with mud and grass to hold them together. When they were done, the Holmes had a farm.

While the others worked, Miss Dorthea sat under a tree and watched the activity carefully. Often, she would call Mary or her mother to fetch her some water, but mostly, she would complain to Master Holmes.

When the house and barn were built, Miss Dorthea took one look and burst into tears. "If I had known Oregon would be as primitive as this, I would have stayed in Louisiana."

"Soon as I can," Master Holmes said, trying to calm her, "I'll ride into town and talk with the banker fella about getting a loan to spruce up the place."

That night, for the first time, Mary's family slept in the barn. Grass had been dried on the floor and made soft bedding. After sleeping under the wagons, lying on the dried grass was like sleeping on a feather bed in the big house.

A few days later, Mary was hanging wash in the yard to dry. Pa and Master Holmes were talking about which crops they would plant for the coming season as a rider came into the yard. He greeted Master Holmes as he got down from his horse.

"Howdy, Mr. Jarred." Master Holmes took his hand and shook it warmly.

"I got your papers, ready to sign. All the terms are right there in the contract." The banker handed the papers to Master Holmes. The master looked from the banker to Pa and then kicked at the dirt on the ground.

"You know," Master Holmes said, "I left my glasses in the cabin. Robin, hold these papers whilst I go fetch `em."

Pa glanced at the papers while Mr. Jarred smoothed the mane on his horse. He reached in his satchel to get some bits of apple when he noticed Pa reading the contract.

"Are you reading those papers, boy?" Mr. Jarred asked.

"Why, no, sir, I can't read," Pa said as Master Holmes returned from the cabin.

"But Pa, you can read real well, write too. You taught me!" Mary blurted out before her father could stop her.

Mr. Jarred turned to Master Holmes. "You wouldn't be letting this boy do your business for you, now would you, Holmes?"

"Heck no." Master Holmes said.

"That's not what this little one says," Mr. Jarred continued.

"Don't mind her. She thinks reading is looking at pictures on a page," Pa said as he cut Mary a sharp look.

"Robin, hand me those papers and we'll finish this business inside." Using the same trick they always used, Pa handed him the papers with the right hand, to signal a good deal. Master Holmes and Mr. Jarred entered the cabin. Pa turned to scold her.

"That was very dangerous, Mary. I told you never to let white folks know what you know," Pa said.

"But I thought things were different here," Mary said.

"They will be," Pa replied.

"But when?" Mary insisted.

"Soon," Pa said, walking away.

Mary returned to her wash. For the first time in her life, she doubted her father's words.

CHAPTER THIRTEEN

That night, Mary's family gathered in the barn, sitting around the wooden table Pa had crafted out of pine trees cleared from the land. Everything they wore, used and ate came from the land. Mary's mother had cooked a fish that Turner had pulled from the stream. It was a strange fish with reddish flesh that Mary had never seen before. Ma said Miss Dorthea called it, "salmon."

"She says it's served in all the fine restaurants in New Orleans," Ma continued. Mary liked the taste of the fish. She liked trying the new things Oregon had to offer.

"We'll harvest plenty this year. But next year, after the ground's seasoned, we'll pull even more," Pa said.

Ma cut him off. "We won't be here next season, Robin. We done everything they asked, built the farm, stored up food. It's time for Master Holmes to free us," Ma said.

"When, Pa, when?" Turner asked.

Pa raised his hand to silence his family. "I promise that tomorrow, we will go to the master and ask him to keep his promise."

The sun had not yet come up the next morning, but Mary was excited. Their first day of freedom had arrived. She washed by the river and dressed early. She hurried to help her mother cook sweet potatoes and corn cakes for their breakfast. Then they went to the Holmes' cabin to start the coffee and cook up biscuits for the Holmes to eat.

Master Holmes and Miss Dorthea were finishing up their breakfast when Pa arrived with Turner.

"Turner, bring in more wood for the fire," Miss Dorthea ordered.

Pa interrupted her. "Beggin' your pardon, Master Holmes, Miss Dorthea, but that ain't why we come."

Mary saw Master Holmes' face grow dark. His eyes got small and the skin around his mouth drew tight. He stood up and faced the family.

"Yes, Robin, I reckon I know what you want," Master Holmes said.

"You made us a promise," Pa said.

"I know what I told you, Robin. And I'm a man of my word. But..." The master hesitated. Miss Dorthea stood next to him and nudged him in the ribs.

"Go on, Tyler, tell them," Miss Dorthea said.

"Since we lost so much on the trail, you and Polly are free," the master started, "but... we're gonna keep the young `uns. They're still our property." Master Holmes dropped his eyes to the floor. Miss Dorthea smiled broadly.

Before Pa could speak, her mother shouted at the master. "You've already taken one child from me; I won't let you have the others!"

"If you don't want to leave your children, Polly, you're welcome to stay on. Lord knows there is plenty of work around here," Miss Dorthea said sweetly.

There was silence for a long time. When Pa finally spoke, his voice was deep and hollow and his hand seemed to tremble.

"We're free. We will not work for you another day without pay," Pa told Master Holmes.

"You know I don't have the money for that, Robin," Master Holmes said.

Pa took her mother's hand and led her to the door. Then he turned to his children. His voice grew softer. It was almost a whisper. "Mary, Turner, we will be back for you. Just wait."

As they walked out the door, Ma cried, "I promise we'll be back."

Miss Dorthea said to her husband. "I don't know how we'll make do running a farm as big as this with just two Negro children to help. You should have found another way to make them stay."

"A promise is a promise, Dorthea. `Sides, we'll be okay. Those children are strong, and the girl can read and write just like her Pa."

"Don't just stand there, girl. Clear this table," Miss Dorthea ordered.

"Go easy on them, Dorthea," Master Holmes said. "They're just children."

Tears streamed down Turner's face. He grabbed Mary around the waist and hugged her for comfort. But there was no one to comfort Mary. She went to the door of the cabin and watched as her mother and father walked to the edge of the Holmes' property and down the dirt road towards freedom.

CHAPTER FOURTEEN

Mary pulled onions from the ground in the noon day sun. Three days had passed since Ma and Pa had left. Mary was afraid she might never see them again.

"Mary, come here right away!" Master Holmes called from the cabin. As Mary ran up the hill, she saw a man ride off the property, but there was no time to watch after him. Master Holmes met her on the doorstep.

Master Holmes shoved some papers in her hands. "What does this say?"

Mary looked at the words. On the top of the page was a circle in ink with raised lettering. It looked like something important. Mary started to read.

"The justice of the Oregon territory of these United States of America orders Mr. Tyler Holmes to report to the twenty-ninth territorial court three days hence, on the thirteenth of September, the year of our Lord, eighteen hundred and fifty-five."

Master Holmes wrinkled his forehead. "Go on, girl."

"You have been named defendant in the case of Holmes vs. McPhedren for the custody of the Negro children, Mary and Turner." When Mary finished reading the papers, she handed them back to Master Holmes. Miss Dorthea came to the door and stood behind the master.

"What does it mean, Tyler?" Miss Dorthea asked.

"That fella from the wagon train, McPhedren, he is taking us to court," the master said. "He's tryin' to take Turner and Mary from us."

Miss Dorthea shuddered. "Why, he didn't buy them from us. He can't do that, can he?"

The master shrugged. "I don't rightly know," he said.

"They were born on our plantation, that makes them ours," she said.

Mary asked quietly, "May I go back to work now, Master Holmes." She could barely contain her excitement.

"Yes, Mary," the master said.

Mary ran down the hill back towards the barn. She was going so fast, she tripped, but she jumped up and continued running.

"Turner, Turner!" Mary cried. She checked inside the barn, but Turner was not there. Mary ran down to the stream, but Turner wasn't there either. Mary ran to the edge of the clearing, where the Holmes farm met the trees. Turner was there chopping wood for the fire.

"Turner," Mary cried, "Mr. McPhedren is taking the master to court, tryin' to get us."

"But, then we'll belong to Mr. McPhedren, not Master Holmes. We still won't be with Ma and Pa, will we?" Turner said.

Turner had more questions than Mary had answers. But all Mary knew was that Pa would keep his promise. They would all be together.

CHAPTER FIFTEEN

When September 13th came around, Master Holmes and Miss Dorthea loaded Mary and Turner on the wagon and drove them into town. Mary and Turner had not left the farm since they arrived in Oregon. As they drew closer, Mary was excited, not only to see her parents, but to see all the sights and sounds that awaited them in the city.

The trial took place in the Calico Saloon, a bar in the center of town. Mary, Turner and the Holmes entered the saloon. The room was crowded with people. They were all talking at once, some were smoking and drinking, too. They were all taller than Mary. She could not see when she tried to search the room for her parents. Miss Alice approached Mary through the crowd.

"Hello, Mary," Miss Alice cooed. Miss Alice was all smiles. Mary thought how good it was to see her again. She ran to give Miss Alice a hug.

"My Charlie's younger brother, Harris McPhedren, will be presenting thy case. Harris is a very good lawyer. Charlie put him through school," Miss Alice told Mary.

"If he wins, does that mean that we belong to you and Mr. McPhedren?" Mary asked.

Miss Alice laughed. "Heavens no! Charlie is taking Mr. Holmes to court because it is against the law for Negroes, Indians and women to sue a white man. My Charlie is suing on behalf of thy father." Miss Alice continued, "If we win, thee and Turner shall be returned to thy parents as the good Lord intended."

"But your God is different than Miss Dorthea's," Mary said. "Her God thinks we should stay with them."

"There is only one God, my child," Miss Alice said. "It is how you hear His word that makes the difference."

Before Mary could consider Miss Alice's words, Miss Dorthea grabbed Mary by the shoulder.

"Come now, we have to get to our seats," Miss Dorthea said. She dragged Mary across the room and away from Miss Alice.

The bailiff called court into session and Judge Williams, a big man with broad shoulders, took the stand. He was the Chief Justice of the Oregon Territorial Supreme Court.

Mary and Turner sat with Miss Dorthea in a section in the back of the room. Mary spotted her mother and father on the other side of the aisle.

"Look Turner, it's Ma and Pa!" Mary said in a whisper. Ma saw her at that very moment and started to cry. She was smiling and crying at the same time. Pa winked at them and then turned his attention to the judge.

Master Holmes and his lawyer sat at one table in front of the judge. Mr. McPhedren and his brother sat at another. Harris McPhedren was thin and tall, with pale skin and light colored hair. His skin was smooth like the back side of a baby. When the judge was seated, he banged his gavel on the bar.

"I call Dorthea Holmes to the stand," said Harris McPhedren.

Miss Dorthea made her way through the crowd to the front of the room and took a seat beside Judge Williams. The bailiff made her swear to tell the truth.

"I always tell the truth," Miss Dorthea answered.

Harris McPhedren approached her. "Mrs. Holmes, were you present when your husband gave his word to Robin to give them their freedom?"

"Yes, against my better judgment," Miss Dorthea replied, "but he didn't say nothin' about those children."

"But he didn't say the offer did not include the children, did he?"

"No," she said.

Harris McPhedren continued, "Don't you think by offering freedom to Robin and Polly, that offer would include their entire family as well?"

Mr. Tate rose. "Your Honor, I object to the prosecution's reference to family. Robin, Polly, Mary and Turner were listed on the farm records as chattel. They are the property of Mr. and Mrs. Tyler Holmes, not a family," Mr. Tate said.

Judge Williams looked at Mary and Turner. Then he looked at Ma and Pa seated across the aisle, separated from them. He turned to Mr. Tate.

"Mr. Tate, does your client, Mr. Holmes, have these records as proof of ownership?" Judge Williams asked.

Master Holmes whispered something in Mr. Tate's ear.

"That's right, he needs proof," a man called from the back row.

"It's his word over a Negro, he don't need nothing," another man said.

"No slavery in the Oregon Territory!" A woman jumped up and yelled.

"Negroes go home," cried another.

Judge Williams banged his gavel. "Order in the court. I want order!"

As the crowd grew quiet, Mr. Tate answered the judge's question. "No, Your Honor, we don't have the records. My client's papers were destroyed on the trail."

"Your Honor, I respectfully submit that Polly and Robin are not property," Harris McPhedren said. "They are a man and a woman seated before you, begging for the custody of their children."

Mr Tate objected. "Mr. McPhedren is appealing to the emotions of this court instead of going by the letter of the law. And the law of this land lists them as property."

"Your objection is sustained," Judge Williams said. "Continue, Mr. McPhedren.

"I'd like to call my next witness, Tyler Holmes," Harris McPhedren said.

The bailiff swore in Master Holmes.

"I swear to tell the whole truth and nothing but the truth. Amen," Master Holmes said and was seated. He held his hat in his hands and twisted it as he spoke. He looked around the room and Mary saw him catch her father's eye.

"Mr. Holmes, did you plan to free Robin, Polly and their children once you arrived in Oregon?" Harris McPhedren asked.

Master Holmes looked down at the floor and spoke. "Well, yes, if we hadn't lost so much on the trail I planned to, but..."

Harris McPhedren interrupted him. "Your Honor, by admitting his original intent, Mr. Holmes has admitted to breaking his agreement to let Robin, Polly and their family go free..."

"Mr. McPhedren overlooks the fact that Mr. Holmes could not possibly make an agreement with Robin because Robin is a slave, a piece of property," Mr. Tate argued. "It would be the same as if he had made a deal with a chicken, a cow or a block of wood. To force him to uphold an agreement like that in court would be absurd."

"Robin Holmes is not a chicken, a cow or a block of wood," Harris McPhedren said. "We are talking about human beings."

"We are talking about slaves," Mr. Tate snapped back.

Harris McPhedren took a piece of paper and handed it to Master Holmes. "Read this to me, please, Mr. Holmes."

Master Holmes tried to read. He stumbled over the words. Mary thought he sounded like she did when she was first learning to read. Mary noticed her master look to her father and then back at the paper. He stopped trying to read, wiped his brow and patted the pockets of his shirt.

"I must've forgot my glasses," Master Holmes said.

"That will be all, Mr. Holmes," Harris McPhedren said. He called Pa forward and handed the paper to him. "Robin, could you read this for me, please?"

"We hold these truths to be self evident, that all men are created equal, endowed by their Creator with the inalienable right to life, liberty and the pursuit of happiness," Pa read. When he finished, he handed the paper back to Harris McPhedren and returned to his seat.

"That was from the Declaration of Independence, written as a governing manifest for this nation, this court, to follow. By denying Robin and Polly the custody of their children, by keeping their flesh in bondage, are we not denying them that which our founding fathers have declared as a God given right - freedom?" Harris McPhedren asked.

Judge Williams rubbed his chin with his hand. Mary could not tell what he was thinking. She only hoped that he would let her live with her parents, let her have the freedom she walked three thousand miles to get.

CHAPTER SIXTEEN

"I rest my case, Your Honor," Harris McPhedren said. He took his seat next to his brother, who smiled encouragingly to Ma and Pa.

The judge spoke. "Mr. Tate, it is your turn to call witnesses."

Mr. Tate stood and looked around the room. His eyes rested on Mary. "I have only one witness, Your Honor. I call the Negro child, Mary, to the stand."

All eyes in the courtroom turned to Mary. Ma squeezed Pa's arm. He whispered in her ear and patted her on the shoulder. Mary wished she knew what he had said to make Ma feel better.

Miss Dorthea pushed Mary from her seat. "Go on, child, you heard the man, go up there."

Mary walked through the crowded courtroom. People whispered as she passed. Mary took a seat next to the judge.

"I object, Your Honor," Mister Harris said, springing from his seat. "She's just a child."

Mary was scared and wished that she had her doll Sadie with her to hold. But when the judge spoke, he made Mary feel better with his words.

"How old are you, child?"

"My Pa says I have nine years," Mary said.

"That's old enough. Go on, Mr. Tate," Judge Williams said. Then he turned to Mary one last time. "Remember child, all you have to do is tell the truth. You know what the truth is, don't you?"

"Yes, sir," Mary said. "My Pa taught me about the truth. He said my life might depend on it someday."

Judge Williams smiled. "Your father must be a wise man."

"Her father is a slave," Mr. Tate reminded the judge, rising from his seat.

"That's enough on that subject, Mr. Tate. Ask your first question," Judge Williams said.

Mr. Tate approached Mary. "What is your name, child?"

Mary answered with the only name she knew. "My name is Mary Holmes."

"And who do you belong to?" Mr. Tate asked.

Mary looked to Miss Dorthea, who gave her a sickly sweet smile. Mary looked to her mother and father, who watched and waited for her answer.

The judge reminded her, "This is very important, Mary. Remember what you told me about the truth."

Mary tried to explain, "I used to live in a cabin on slave row with my Ma and my Pa and my little brother, Turner. My Ma cooked us good meals even when there wasn't much to eat. And my Pa, he always took care of us, and always made sure we stayed together. I love them and I like my little brother even though he plays the fiddle bad."

There was laughter in the courtroom as Mr. Tate interrupted her. "Answer the question. Who do you belong to?"

Mary swallowed and said, "I belong to Master Holmes and Miss Dorthea."

Mr. Tate threw up his arms. "Your Honor, the child stated that she belongs to her master, Tyler Holmes. She is and considers herself to be his property. I submit this as proof of ownership by my client. I rest my case."

Mary looked around the room. She saw Ma bury her head in Pa's shoulder. Mary saw Miss Dorthea grinning while Mr. Tate and Master Holmes shook hands. The courtroom grew loud with talking as people for and against the case complained.

Judge Williams leaned back in his chair. Mary watched the judge as he looked from her to Turner to her Ma and Pa. Then he banged his gavel on the bar and shouted above the crowd.

"Silence! I have my verdict," the judge said. "I would be glad to rule in favor of Mr. Holmes if he had the proper evidence to prove that these here children belong to him. But the only evidence he has is the word of a Negro child. And we all know that the testimony of a Negro cannot be admitted in a United States court of law." Judge Williams smiled at Mary and continued. "In that case, I must in all good conscience, award custody of Mary and Turner to Mr. Charles McPhedren. Court is dismissed!"

Ma ran to Turner and hugged him while Pa rushed to the front of the room. He took Mary in his arms and swung her high into the air. Then he gave her a big bear hug.

"We won, Mary. You and Turner can live with us now," he said.

Ma brought Turner to the front of the room. They were all together again, the whole family. Miss Alice, Mr. McPhedren and his brother joined them.

"Harris," Mr. McPhedren said, "I am very proud of thee."

"Yes, sir, thank you for your help," Pa said. He took Harris McPhedren's hand and shook it.

"I wish I could take all the credit, Robin," Harris McPhedren said. "But Mary was a big help. She showed the judge that you folks really are a family."

Master Holmes approached. "Robin," he said, "I just want you to know that...what I'm tryin' to say is...if it weren't for what we lost on the trail and Dorthea pushin' me and all...well, what I mean is...you're a good man, Robin. I always thought that. Not chattel or property, but a man. What I'm trying to say is..." The master hesitated, looked at the ground for a moment and then spoke again. "Sometimes it takes getting to see a real man to make a fella act like one." Master Holmes extended his hand to Pa. "Shake?"

Pa looked at Master Holmes long and hard. Finally, he took Master Holmes hand and shook it. Not as a slave, but as an equal.

Then without a word, Pa took his children by the hand and led them away from where Master Holmes stood.

Mary turned to her father. "I'm free now, but I'm not sure I feel any different," Mary said. "Is this what freedom feels like?"

"Freedom is whatever you make of it, Sunshine," Pa said.

CHAPTER SEVENTEEN

Mary and her family moved into the McPhedrens' cabin while they built their own home on a grant of land next door. It was hard work, but somehow Mary was never so tired these days as she had been when she worked for Master Holmes.

On the day they raised the roof, they held a party to celebrate that was better than any party Mary had ever seen back on the plantation.

"I'm so happy, I don't care if Turner plays the same songs forever," Mary said as she danced with Mr. McPhedren.

"But I won't," Turner said. "I been practicing a new one Mr. Harris showed me."

"You play the fiddle?" Pa asked him.

"One of the many things I was able to study in school thanks to my good brother's assistance," Harris McPhedren answered. "Show them what you can do, Turner."

Turner broke into a rousing version of a song Mary had never heard. She turned to Mr. McPhedren and tried dancing anyway. Then Pa cut in.

"Would you mind, Friend Charlie?" Pa said.

"Not at all, Friend Robin," Mr. McPhedren said as he stepped aside to let Mary dance with her father. Halfway through the song, there was a knock at the door.

Miss Alice answered it. "Hello," she said. "May I help you?"

"Excuse me, Ma'am, but we were looking for the McPhedren place?" a voice came from the dark. It was a familiar voice to Mary.

"You've found it, friend," Mr. McPhedren said. "Come in."

"Buddy!" Mary cried as she saw him enter the cabin. Uncle Jasper was right behind him. Mary and her family surrounded them.

"What happened?" Ma asked.

"We took you for dead," Turner said.

"It was what Bostwick told us," Pa said. He touched his chin when he said it. It reminded Mary of the beating he took the night Bostwick brought them the news. "Said they found two slaves dead at the creek."

"They might have, sure," Uncle Jasper said.

"Those other runaways bushwhacked us and took the pass Mary wrote us," Buddy said, accepting a hug from Ma. "It was those men must've died crossing the river."

"After that, we left the main roads and took to the woods traveling by night for the whole of the trip," Uncle Jasper explained.

"That probably saved your lives," Pa said.

"We done made it north and joined a wagon train," Uncle Jasper said. "Praying all the way we'd find you here."

"And the Lord listened," Mr. McPhedren said.

"And the Lord answered," Miss Alice added.

"Friend Charlie, Miss Alice," Pa said. "This is Buddy and Uncle Jasper."

Mr. McPhedren held out his hand to them. "Welcome to our home."

Uncle Jasper hesitated. Mary knew he had never before been offered the hand of a white man. But Buddy stepped forward and shook firmly. Mary smiled. He would do well in this new life.

"I must say, that's a sight that warms my soul," Uncle Jasper said.

"I have other news might do the same," Ma said quietly. She took Pa's hand and faced the family. "After all these years... there's another baby on the way."

"Polly, really?" Miss Alice asked.

"Oh, Mama," Mary blurted out. "Please, please, can we name her Freedom?"

"How you know it'll be a girl?" Turner asked.

"It doesn't matter," Pa said, quieting them. "Boy or girl, they'll be free. And that's what's important."

"Freedom, eh? Well, maybe we can call her Frieda for short," Ma said.

"Uncle Jasper," Mary said, tugging his hand. "Remember when you told us about your great-grandparents being free?"

"Yes, Mary," Uncle Jasper said, squeezing her hand.

"Now we all know what freedom's like," Mary said proudly.

"Yes, Mary," Uncle Jasper said. "Now we do."

About the story

The Promise is a historical fiction, inspired by Holmes vs. Ford, a landmark legal case which helped the people of Oregon decide if they would come into the Union as a slave state or a free state.

For links to historical information about the Holmes vs. Ford case, see http://welchwrite.com/Promise

Made in the USA
Middletown, DE
09 January 2019